Antoinette Portis

Princess Super Kitty

HARPER
An Imprint of HarperCollinsPublishers

There are girls who are regular girls.
But not me. I have ears and a tail.
Because today I am a kitty!

When Mom says, "Maggie,"
I say, "Meow."
That means "I am a kitty, not a Maggie."

Kitties are cuter than regular people.

When Mom says, "Milk or juice?"
I say, "Meow."

That means "Milk, please."

Kitties only drink milk. From a dish.

Then Mom says, "Are you hungry, Kitty?"
And I say, "Meow." That means "Yes."

Kitties only eat fish.

And peanut butter and banana sandwiches.

Kitties like to take lots of naps.

But not me.

Because I'm not just a kitty,

I am a Super Kitty!

Super Kitties don't take naps.
They fly all over the place

and look for people to rescue.

When Mom says, "Super Kitty,
can you bring me the baby's bottle?"

I say, "Yes!" And zoom there
in zero seconds.

Super Kitties can see things with their superstrong eyes.

They lift things with their superstrong muscles.

AND Super Kitties have to open jars
for everybody in the whole world.

But not me.

Because I'm not just super and a kitty,

I am a *Princess* Super Kitty!

Princess Super Kitties do not open jars.
They do royal things. With jewels.

Sometimes Princess Super Kitties let their brothers play with them.

"Glue stick, please!"

A Princess Super Kitty is someone you obey.

Princess Super Kitties make parades around the land so their people can adore them.

"Hi, Mom."

I love being a Princess Super Kitty!

Then Mom says, "It's bath time, Princess Super Kitty!"

Princess Super Kitties don't like baths.
They run and hide.

But not me—
I don't run and hide.

Because now I'm not just a Princess
and Super and a Kitty—

I am a Water Lily Hula Porpoise
Princess Super Kitty of the Sea!

Meow.

For Edward, Colman, Celia, and Will.

We had fun.

Library of Congress Cataloging-in-Publication Data

Portis, Antoinette.
  Princess Super Kitty / Antoinette Portis. — 1st ed.
    p. cm.
  Summary: Maggie, a little girl with a huge imagination, becomes a cat, a superhero, a princess, and more
in the course of a day.
  ISBN 978-0-06-182725-9 (trade bdg.) — ISBN 978-0-06-182726-6 (lib. bdg.)
  [1. Imagination—Fiction.] I. Title.
PZ7.P8362Pri 2011   2010032230
[E]—dc22   CIP
                                                                                        AC

Typography by Martha Rago
12 13 14 15 LPR 10 9 8 7 6 5 4 3
❖
First Edition